To families everywhere who have made my books a part of
their children's lives. I am honored and words
cannot suffice. Thank you.
—K. W.

For Dylan
—J. C.

Margaret K. McElderry Books • An imprint of Simon & Schuster Children's Publishing Division •
1230 Avenue of the Americas, New York, New York 10020 • Text copyright © 2009 by
Karma Wilson • Illustrations copyright © 2009 by Jane Chapman • All rights reserved,
including the right of reproduction in whole or in part in any form. • Book design by
Krista Vossen • The text for this book is set in Tarzana Narrow. • The illustrations
for this book are rendered in acrylic. • Manufactured in China • 10 9 8 7 6 5 4 3 •
Library of Congress Cataloging-in-Publication Data • Wilson, Karma. Don't be afraid, Little
Pip / Karma Wilson ; illustrated by Jane Chapman. — 1st ed. • p. cm. • Summary: Afraid
to swim, Pip the penguin would much rather learn to fly. • ISBN 978-0-689-85987-8 •
[1. Fear—Fiction. 2. Swimming—Fiction. 3. Penguins—Fiction.] • I. Chapman, Jane, 1970- ill. II.
Title. III. Title: Do not be afraid, Little Pip. • PZ7.W69656Do 2009 • [E]—dc22 • 2007041745

Don't Be Afraid, Little Pip

Karma Wilson illustrated by **Jane Chapman**

Margaret K. McElderry Books
New York London Toronto Sydney

Little Pip looked out at the large ocean. Today was the day all young penguins were learning how to swim.

Pip sighed. The ocean looked awfully dark and deep. She gazed up. The blue sky looked bright and cheerful. *I think I'd much rather fly than swim,* she thought.

FLIP, FLAP . . .   **FLIP, FLAP . . .**

Mama and Papa waddled up.
"It's your big day, Pip," said Papa.
"Aren't you excited?"

"You are growing up, little one," Mama said
with a smile. "Soon you will be swimming
with all the other youngsters. What fun
you will have!"

Pip frowned. "But I'm a bird. And birds fly."
She pointed to the seagulls circling above.

Mama laughed. "Don't be afraid, Little Pip.
Penguins don't fly, they swim. That's what
makes us special."

And Mama and Papa sang:

"Into the water, under the sea—
that's the best place for a penguin to be.
Flapping our wings and swishing on by.
Penguins can swim, so why should we fly?"

Pip did not sing along.
She looked up again at the sky.
"I still just want to fly," she whispered.

Soon all of the young penguins were gathered at the shore.
Their teacher, Mr. Tucks, cautioned, "Do not wander, younglings.
Swimming is an art and you must learn properly."

A penguin sidled up to Pip. "I can't
wait! Can you?" she squeaked. "Hi!
I'm Merry. What's your name?"

Pip mumbled her name.

"Hello, Pip," Merry gushed. "Swimming! This will be the best day of our lives! Aren't you excited?"

Pip shook her head. "Aren't you a little bit scared? What's under there, in the dark?"

"Oh, all sorts of wonderful things," said Merry, "like a huge octopus, coral forests, and giant sea plants."

Pip shivered. "That doesn't help."

"We are penguins," said Merry,
"and all penguins swim, you know.
I'll be right by your side, okay?"

"We are birds," said Pip.
"Shouldn't birds fly?"

Merry laughed. "Not penguin birds, silly."

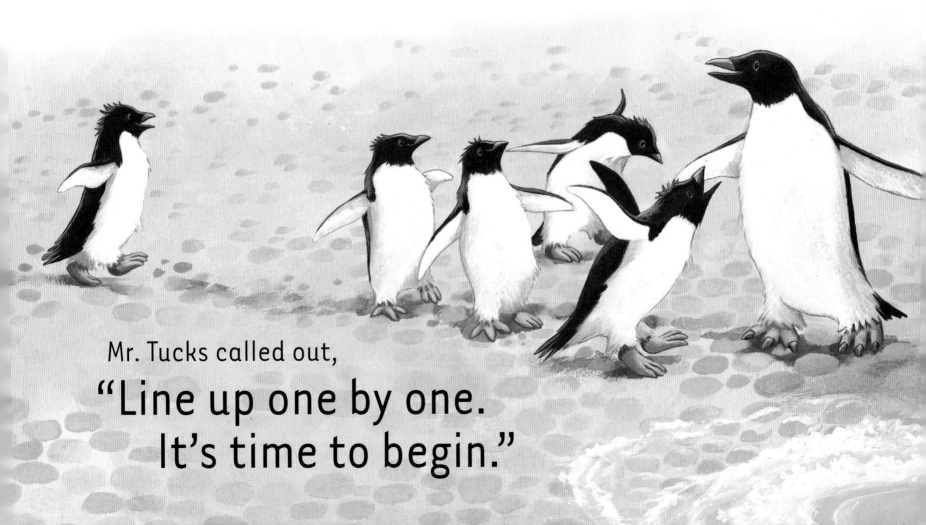

Mr. Tucks called out,
"Line up one by one.
It's time to begin."

In all the excitement, Little Pip slipped away. "No swimming for me," she said.

FLAP, FLAP, SLAP.

She wandered away down the shoreline.

I can learn to fly, thought Pip. *I just need some help.*

Ahead, Pip saw a Snow Petrel.

"She can help!" cried Pip,
racing toward the big bird.

"Hello. I want to fly.
Can you help me?"

The petrel looked at Pip. "You look like a penguin to me. Don't know if you've heard, but penguins *don't* fly."

Pip pointed to her new glossy feathers. "I have wings," she said. "I am a bird, too, so I can fly."

The petrel pondered. "Well, that's true.
Wings and feathers! Maybe you *can* fly."
And so she sang:

"*Pick up your feet, run down the shore.
Flap your wings and flap some more.
Lift up your beak, look to the sky.
Take a leap and FLY, FLY, FLY!*"

"Oh, thank you," said Pip.
"That will help!"

Pip ran.

Pip flapped.

She leaped and . . .

Pip flapped some more.

PLOP . . .

Pip fell. Her beak was full of sand.

"Oh, well," said the petrel kindly. "I told you, dear, penguins don't fly." And away the petrel flew, far out over the ocean.

Pip sighed. "Why do I even have wings?"

She waddled on until she came to another bird, this one black and white just like a penguin.

But it wasn't a penguin. It was a majestic Giant Albatross.

"Hello. Can you help me? I want to fly."

The albatross chuckled. "And I want to dive deep into the ocean and swim for hours," he said. "But I cannot, no more than penguins can fly."

Pip frowned. "You have black wings. So do I. We are not so very different."

The albatross shook his head. "Well,
you are determined, I'll give you that.
Let's see now . . ." And then he sang:

"Stand on a ledge by the edge of the sea.
Let your feathers set you free.
Lift your wings and spread them wide.
Jump into the breeze and away you'll glide!"

"Oh, thank you," said Pip.
"That will help!"

"Good luck," said the albatross,
and he glided away on the wind.

Pip found a ledge. It was not too big, just small enough for her first jump.

Pip climbed.

Pip spread her wings.

Pip jumped and . . .

SPLASH!

Oh, no! Pip had fallen right into the cold, dark sea!

"COUGH!" GURGLE! SPUTTER! Pip flailed about, choking on the water.

"HELP!" she cried. *GURGLE!*

"HELP ME!" *SPUTTER!*

Pip's face slipped under the water . . .

then she felt something grab
hold of her . . .

and push her up into the air!

It was Merry!

"What are you doing, Pip?" said Merry. "You're not swimming, that's for sure!"

"I wanted to fly," said Pip.

Merry laughed. "Well, you're in the water, so you'd better swim now. I can't keep holding you up like this. So, take a deep breath, kick your feet, and flap your wings. It's easy! I'll help you."

Merry gave Pip a gentle nudge back into the waves.

Pip held her breath.

Pip kicked.

Pip SWAM!

Pip flapped and . . .

Deep under the water and into the dark blue sea
went Pip. *Whooosh! Whiiiish! Wheeeeee!!*
She swooped past a huge octopus, beautiful
coral reefs, and giant sea plants. She saw
schools of fish as bright as a rainbow in the sky.

Pip came up for air. "Thank you, Merry!" she cried. "I'm flying after all! **Swimming IS flying!**"

Darting and dashing, splishing and splashing through the waves, Pip and Merry swam together all the way back to shore.

When Mama saw Pip, she smiled, and Papa said, "Little Pip, you can swim!"

They snuggled together and then Pip sang this song:

"Into the water, under the sea—
that's the best place for a penguin to be.
Flapping our wings and swishing on by.
Now I can swim and now I can fly!"